NO MALTO LEFT BEHIND!

By Ryder Windham
Illustrated by Patrick Spaziante

Simon Spotlight
New York   London   Toronto   Sydney   New Delhi

If you purchase this book without a cover, you should be aware that this book is stolen property. It was reported as "unsold and destroyed" to the publisher, and neither the author nor the publisher has received any payment for this "stripped book."

This book is a work of fiction. Any references to historical events, real people, or real places are used fictitiously. Other names, characters, places, and events are products of the author's imagination, and any resemblance to actual events or places or persons, living or dead, is entirely coincidental.

SIMON SPOTLIGHT
An imprint of Simon & Schuster Children's Publishing Division
1230 Avenue of the Americas, New York, New York 10020
This Simon Spotlight edition May 2024
TRANSFORMERS and HASBRO and all related trademarks and logos are trademarks of Hasbro, Inc. © 2024 Hasbro. Transformers: EarthSpark TV series © 2024 Hasbro/Viacom International Inc. All Rights Reserved.
Nickelodeon is a trademark of Viacom International Inc.
All rights reserved, including the right of reproduction in whole or in part in any form.
SIMON SPOTLIGHT and colophon are registered trademarks of Simon & Schuster, LLC.
Simon & Schuster: Celebrating 100 Years of Publishing in 2024
For information about special discounts for bulk purchases, please contact Simon & Schuster Special Sales at 1-866-506-1949 or business@simonandschuster.com.
Designed by Sarah Richards Taylor
The illustrations for this book were rendered digitally.
The text of this book was set in Proxima Nova.
Manufactured in the United States of America 0324 OFF
10 9 8 7 6 5 4 3 2 1
ISBN 978-1-6659-5185-2 (hc)
ISBN 978-1-6659-5184-5 (pbk)
ISBN 978-1-6659-5186-9 (ebook)

CONTENTS

CHAPTER 1	THE MALTO MISSION	**1**
CHAPTER 2	SECRET MOTIVES	**13**
CHAPTER 3	PRIVATE PROPERTY	**25**
CHAPTER 4	A TRAINING DISASTER	**37**
CHAPTER 5	TEAM MALTO	**49**

CHAPTER 1
THE MALTO MISSION

Standing next to the Transformers robot Bumblebee, Dot Malto faced her seven children and said, "Listen up, Maltos. Optimus Prime has given us a mission!"

The Malto children included Mo, her brother Robby, and their Terran siblings: Twitch, Thrash, Hashtag, Nightshade, and Jawbreaker. They had been playing tag outside the large barn on their family's farm, but now they gave their full attention to their mother and Bumblebee. Their father, Alex Malto, stepped out of the house and asked, "What's going on?"

Bumblebee said, "Optimus Prime

believes that one of Mandroid's Arachnamechs is on the loose and possibly hiding in some nearby woods. He wants us to track the Arachnamech and, if possible, capture it."

"Wow!" Mo got excited. "We're going on a real mission!"

"Hang on," Alex Malto said. He looked at Dot. "Two of our children have book reports that are due tomorrow."

Dot frowned as she turned to Robby and Mo. "I'm sorry, but you know the family rules about schoolwork. You'll have to stay here with Dad."

"But that's not fair!" Robby said. "If the Terrans can go on a mission with you, Mo and I should be able to go too!"

Dot shook her head. "No, your education comes first. And today, finishing homework is your mission."

On their arms, Robby and Mo wore Cyber-Sleeves, devices that emotionally connected them with the Terrans. As the Cyber-Sleeves glowed blue, Hashtag said, "Whoa. I feel like I just got splashed by a wave of sadness."

"We're all feeling it," Twitch said. Turning to Mo and Robby, she said, "This mission probably won't take long. Try to finish your book reports before we get back, and then we'll have more time to play."

"Speaking of time," Bumblebee said, "let's not waste any!" He rapidly changed into his sleek yellow sports car alt mode. Dot climbed into her park ranger truck. Twitch quickly converted into her fierce red drone alt mode. Thrash switched into his silver motorcycle alt mode and positioned himself next to Bumblebee, who revved his engine, ready to race off. Hashtag converted into her surveillance van alt mode. Nightshade quickly changed into their mighty owl alt mode, as Jawbreaker converted into his Stygimoloch alt mode and readied his claws into the ground, prepared to leap through the forest. Bumblebee tore out of the driveway, followed by Dot's truck and the Terrans.

Watching the convoy take off, Robby said, "We've literally been left behind!"

"Yeah," Mo agreed, "Terrans have all the fun!"

"Fun?!" Alex said. "The Terrans are tracking an enemy robot, but you two make it sound like they're off playing games without you. And is it the Terrans' fault that your homework isn't finished?"

Mo sighed. "No, Dad."

"It's our own fault," Robby said.

"Hey, here's an idea that may make you happy," Alex said. "While you do homework, how about I cook up a batch of Filipino *lumpia*?"

"I love *lumpia*!" Mo said.

As Robby and Mo followed Alex into the house, Robby leaned close to Mo and whispered, "I know a way we can help the Terrans and also get our homework done faster."

"Really?" Mo whispered back.

"Really," Robby said. "Wait until you hear my idea!"

CHAPTER 2
SECRET MOTIVES

"I wish Mo and Robby were with us," Jawbreaker yelled up to Nightshade, who was effortlessly keeping up with Jawbreaker's nimble alt mode.

"I do too," Nightshade said. "But we're only a little over a mile from home. The sooner we wrap up this mission, the sooner we'll be back with Mo and Robby!"

Bumblebee came to a sudden stop,

and the others quickly halted beside him. Dot Malto jumped out of her truck as the Terrans all gathered next to her. Looking around, the Terrans saw that Dot had parked her truck on

an old path in a wooded area near a long limestone outcrop, not far from the road. Bumblebee changed to his bot mode and stepped over beside the Terrans.

"As you all know," Bumblebee began to explain, "Mandroid created Arachnamechs to serve him. They have limited intelligence, but they're fast and quite powerful. To find one, we have to move quietly and keep our optical and audio sensors wide open."

"I'll use my eyes and ears," Dot said. "While we're searching, keep your radio comms on, and contact Bumblebee and me if you see any sign of an Arachnamech. Understood?"

"Understood, Mom!" Hashtag said as she saluted Dot.

Leaving Dot's truck parked beside

the long rock formation, the group fanned out but stayed within sight of each other as they moved through the woods. Birds chirped and whistled from the surrounding trees, while the Terrans, Dot, and Bumblebee looked for broken branches, tracks on the ground, lost pieces of metal, and any other evidence of an enemy robot.

Thirteen minutes later, a lone robot lifted its dark, bulbous head from its hiding spot behind the rock formation near the parked vehicle. Rising onto its six legs, the robot moved silently over to the truck. Looking down at the ground, the robot's six eyes glowed bright red as it examined the various tire tracks, including Bumblebee's. The robot followed the tracks to the

road, and its head made a soft clicking noise as it determined the direction that Bumblebee, Dot, and the Terrans had come from.

Staying off the road and out of sight, the Arachnamech skittered through the woods and across fields of high grass as it proceeded toward the Malto family farm.

Clutching a notebook along with a paperback edition of *Treasure Island*, by Robert Louis Stevenson, Robby stepped into Mo's bedroom, saw her seated at her desk, and said, "Grab your school stuff and come with me."

Mo grabbed her own notebook and paperback. As she followed Robby into the hallway, she whispered, "Tell me your idea."

"Do you remember Nightshade's invention, the Smart Trainer 5007?"

Mo frowned. "How could I forget a flying ball that nearly zapped us?"

"But Nightshade made lots of test models for the Smart Trainer," Robby said as they went downstairs. "I'm sure we can fix one to help the Terrans with their training exercises and help us with our homework."

Mo said, "You think you can fix a Smart Trainer? This is going to be interesting!"

CHAPTER 3
PRIVATE PROPERTY

Carrying their schoolwork, Mo and Robby went into the kitchen, where their father was busily preparing *lumpia*. "Hey, Dad," Robby said. "Is it okay if Mo and I do our book reports in the Dugout?"

"Go right ahead!" Alex said. "Snacks will be ready in about ten minutes."

As Mo and Robby walked from the house to the barn, Mo whispered,

"This is your worst idea ever."

"Oh yeah?" Robby asked. "Then why are you tagging along?"

"To make sure you don't get hurt!" Mo said.

Inside the barn, they entered a secret staircase that led down to the Dugout, a series of underground chambers Nightshade created for the Terrans. Mo hesitantly led the way. "Did you forget that Nightshade named the Smart Trainer 5007 after the first one, 5006, tried to destroy them, and after that number 5007 malfunctioned too?" she said.

"So they made a few mistakes!"

Robby said, brushing past Mo and entering Nightshade's laboratory. "But did you forget that Nightshade also equipped the Smart Trainer with the latest adaptive artificial intelligence, and that it can talk? That means it can learn how to do book reports and tell us what to write."

Mo gasped. "But that's cheating!"

"No it's not," Robby said as he placed his paperback and notebook on a workbench. "The Smart Trainer will just be helping us, like a tutor. And by testing it, we'll be helping the Terrans." Robby looked at a shelf above the workbench and found a small metal ball covered with sensors, propulsion systems, and a single green button. He grinned as he picked up the ball. "We are so in luck!" He held out the ball so Mo could see the number etched on it.

"Number 5008?" Mo asked him. "Robby, put it back."

"But it must be the newest model!" Robby said. "I'll bet Nightshade installed better safety features in this one." Before Mo could protest, Robby pressed the Smart Trainer's green button. The Smart Trainer glowed as it rose out of Robby's hand and hovered in the air.

"Greetings, Maltobots," the Smart Trainer said, but then it readjusted its optical sensor to study the children. "Correction... you are not Maltobots."

"Hey, 5008!" Robby said. "We're Robby and Mo Malto, and we want you to help us do our homework, and—"

"You are trespassing on private property," the Smart Trainer interrupted. "Trespassers will be removed from here. By force if necessary."

"Trespassers?" Robby asked. "But we're not—"

As the Smart Trainer began to charge its systems, Mo grabbed Robby's wrist and shouted, "Run for the stairs!"

Back in the forest, the Arachnamech crept quickly past the trees along the edge of the road until it arrived at an unpaved driveway. Examining the dirt, the Arachnamech recognized

Bumblebee's tracks. Looking up the driveway, the Arachnamech saw a house and a red barn.

It stayed low as it skulked toward the buildings.

CHAPTER 4
A TRAINING DISASTER

Inside the Dugout, Mo started to tug a very startled Robby up the stairs. The Smart Trainer fired a beam of energy that smashed into the floor near Robby's feet. As they got farther up the stairs and approached the barn, Robby and Mo heard more blasts from the Smart Trainer.

"You were right, Mo!" Robby shouted. "Worst idea ever!"

Over a mile away from the Malto family farm, Bumblebee, Dot, and the Terrans had just returned to Dot's truck when the Terrans' eyes suddenly glowed with great intensity. Twitch said, "I . . . I feel frightened."

Thrash glanced at his Terran siblings. "We're all feeling it," he said, "because . . ."

"Mo and Robby are in danger!" Nightshade finished.

Just then Jawbreaker noticed strange footprints on the ground behind Dot's truck. He said, "Are these Arachnamech tracks?"

"They are," Bumblebee said, "and they lead to the road!" He shifted his body parts and instantly changed to his sports car alt mode.

"Let's get home," Dot said. "And fast!"

Running full speed up the stairs, Mo

and Robby tumbled out into the barn. As they ran for a door that led outside, the Smart Trainer launched energy beams up through the staircase, taking the door to the stairs off its hinges. The Smart Trainer rose fast through the hole and set its target on the fleeing children.

Mo darted through the door and into the driveway. Before Robby could follow her out, the Smart Trainer fired from behind. Robby jumped sideways to avoid the energy blast that whizzed past him. He landed on his back and leaned against the barn to catch his breath. As the Smart

Trainer recharged, Robby stood up, activated his Cyber-Sword, and swung ferociously; the Smart Trainer was sent flying through the open barn window.

Mo was halfway across the driveway, running toward the house, when she heard a loud *bang* come from the barn. She glanced over her shoulder and saw that the Smart Trainer was now swooping overhead.

Robby, with his Cyber-Sword now deactivated, stepped out of the barn and yelled, "Mo! Behind you!"

Mo turned to see an Arachnamech crouched on the grass in the shadow of the house. The Arachnamech sprang toward Mo, but she dropped, rolled across the ground, and came to a stop next to a garden hose. Thinking fast, Mo turned on the water tap as she picked up the spray nozzle attached to the end of the hose. The Arachnamech was preparing to pounce again when Mo squeezed the nozzle's handle and sent a powerful stream of water at her opponent.

Mo continued spraying the Arachnamech while Robby used his CyberShield to deflect the Smart Trainer's energy blasts. As Robby moved closer to Mo, the Smart Trainer noticed the soaking-wet Arachnamech.

"A fellow robot is under attack!" the Smart Trainer said. "I shall assist

it in defeating the trespassers!"

At that moment, Alex opened the kitchen door and stepped out. Smiling as he carried a loaded tray of *lumpia*, he said, "Anyone hungry?" Then he saw the two menacing robots and said, "Uh-oh."

CHAPTER 5
TEAM MALTO

"Dad, help!" Robby said.

Alex threw his tray of *lumpia* at the hovering Smart Trainer. He tried to kick the Arachnamech, but Mo accidentally sprayed him and he slipped and fell on the wet grass.

The Smart Trainer, now partially covered with ingredients from the *lumpia*, rotated fast in midair to shake off bits of bean sprouts and garlic.

As Alex pushed himself up from the ground, the Arachnamech flexed one of its sharp legs and cut through Mo's garden hose. Robby, now with his Cyber-Sword reactivated, swung at the Smart Trainer but missed. The Smart Trainer weaved and prepared to blast again. Quickly, Mo activated her Cyber-Shield, ready to defend her family.

An approaching car's loud engine caused the Smart Trainer and the Arachnamech to turn their attention to the driveway. They saw Bumblebee racing toward them in his swift alt mode. Dot's truck and the Terrans were not far behind him.

Bumblebee skidded to a stop as Dot and the Terrans quickly halted in the swirling dust of the dirt driveway. The Arachnamech sprang at Bumblebee. Bumblebee shifted into his bot mode and hit the Arachnamech so hard that it cracked into pieces.

The Smart Trainer swooped toward Dot and said, "Another trespasser!"

But before the Smart Trainer could do anything, Jawbreaker, now in his extremely large bot mode, reached out, grabbed it, and crushed it with a loud crunch between his massive fingers.

Bumblebee said, "Nightshade, wasn't that one of your inventions?"

"Indeed," Nightshade confirmed. "It's the Smart Trainer 5008!"

"Mo and Robby!" Twitch said. "We sensed you were in danger!"

Thrash continued, "Not only that, but Bumblebee guessed that Arachnamech was heading here, so—"

"So our tracking mission led us back home!" Hashtag finished.

Nightshade asked, "How did the Smart Trainer 5008 get out of the Dugout?"

"That was all my fault," Robby

admitted. "I . . . I thought maybe I could get it to help me do homework faster, and then Mo and I could spend more time with our siblings."

"It's my fault too," Mo said. "I tried to stop Robby, but I didn't try hard enough."

Dot sighed. "I'm sorry you two felt so left out."

"We're sorry too," Robby said. "Nightshade, I'm also sorry I switched on your Smart Trainer without permission."

"And I'm sorry," Nightshade said, "that I didn't disassemble it after I realized it was hazardous."

"Excuse me," Jawbreaker said, "but before anyone else apologizes, maybe we should keep in mind that even though some of us were in different places today, we were always thinking of each other. And working together, we did find the Arachnamech."

"True!" Bumblebee said. "I'll inform Optimus Prime at once."

"Mo and Robby," Twitch began. "Schoolwork might prevent you from going on every mission with us, but even when we're apart, your support and encouragement always helps us!"

"From now on," Dot said, "no Malto should ever feel left behind."

"Robby and I had better get cracking on our book reports so we won't feel left behind at school, either," Mo added.

"And I'll get cracking on cleaning the yard," Alex said as he gestured at the scattered remains of enemy robots and *lumpia*. "Ready, team?"

The Malto family all placed one hand in the center of their family circle.

"Ready team . . . break!"

Ready for another **TRANSFORMERS EARTHSPARK** adventure?

Here's a sneak peek of Book 3,

MAY THE BEST BOT WIN!

The next day, while Robby and Mo were at school and Bumblebee was on his mission, the five Terrans walked up to Wheeljack as he repaired an old tractor in the barn. Seeing the Terrans, Wheeljack set aside his tools and said, "Something on your minds, kids?"

"Yesterday," Nightshade said, "we learned about sibling rivalry. My Terran siblings and I believe we might benefit from competing with each other. Because you are a scientist, we trust you to design a competition that tests our athleticism, intelligence, and creativity."

"A competition with three tests?" Wheeljack said. "That's called a triathlon. Do all of you want to compete?"